I'M EXCITED

DEALING WITH FEELINGS

I'M EXCITED

Written by Elizabeth Crary   Illustrated by Jean Whitney

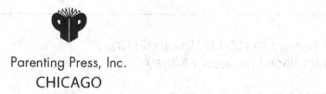

Parenting Press, Inc.

CHICAGO

Why a Book on Feeling Excited?

Parents often ask me for help dealing with their children's feelings. This may be because many people were taught to ignore their feelings as children. Now they want to raise their own children differently, but have no idea how.

How can this book help?

I'm Excited can help children accept their feelings and decide how to respond.

The book models a constructive process for handling feelings. It shows a parent and child discussing feelings openly. The story also offers specific options for children. There are verbal, physical, and creative ways described to express feelings. In addition, *I'm Excited* serves as a role model for parents who wish to change the way they respond to their children's feelings.

How to use *I'm Excited*

I'm Excited becomes more useful with time and repetition. A couple of readings probably won't make a dramatic change. But you can start to help your child transfer the information to real life.

Distinguish between feelings and actions. Read the book, letting the child choose the options. Ask, "How do Annie and Jessie *feel* now? What will they *do* next?" at the end of each page.

Introduce different options. Children need several ways to cope with feelings that work for them. This story offers ten ideas. When you are done reading, ask your child, "What else could Annie and Jesse have done?" Record your child's responses on the "Idea Page" at the end.

Use as a springboard for discussing other situations. Begin by discussing something that happened to someone else. Ask your child to identify the feelings and the alternatives the child tried. Talk with your child from the perspective of collecting information, rather than what is right or wrong.

For example, assume a visiting friend, Mike, did not want to go home. Ask, "How did Mike *feel* when it was time to go home?" "What did he do first when he felt upset?" "What else did he do?" Possible answers might be: he ignored the request, he said "No", or he scowled and said "Okay."

When your child can distinguish between feelings and behavior for other people, you can review something he did in the same nonjudgmental way.

Elizabeth Crary, Seattle, Washington

Copyright © 1994 by Elizabeth Crary
Illustrations by Jean Whitney

ISBN 978-0-943990-91-0
LC 93-085378

Parenting Press, Inc.
814 North Franklin Street
Chicago, Illinois 60610
www.ParentingPress.com

Feelings and the Parent's Role

One of your jobs as a parent or teacher is to help children understand and deal with their feelings. Children need basic information about feelings, they need to have their feelings validated, and they need to have tools to deal with those feelings. These are discussed below.

1. Develop a vocabulary.

Children may feel overwhelmed by intense feelings. One simple way to begin understanding feelings is to label them.

- Share your feelings: "I feel frustrated when I spill coffee on the floor."
- Read books that discuss feelings, like the *Let's Talk About Feelings* series.
- Observe another's feelings: "I'll bet he's proud of that A+ grade."

In addition, introduce your child to different words for related feelings—for example, mad, furious, angry, upset, etc.

2. Help children distinguish between feelings and actions.

Understand that feelings are neither good nor bad. Feeling mad is neither good nor bad. However, hitting is a behavior. Hitting is not acceptable. You can say, "It's okay to be mad, but I cannot let you hit your sister."

3. Validate the child's feelings.

Many people have been trained to ignore or suppress their feelings. Girls are often taught that being mad is unfeminine or not nice. Boys are taught not to cry. You can validate children's feelings by listening to them and reflecting the feeling. Listen without judging. Remain separate.

Remember, your child's feelings belong to her/him.

When you reflect the feeling ("You are mad that Stephanie has to go home now"), you are not attempting to solve the problem. Reflecting, or acknowledging the feeling helps the child deal with it.

4. Offer children several ways to cope with their feelings.

If telling children to "Use your words" worked for most kids, grown-ups would have little trouble with children's feelings. Children need a variety of ways to respond—auditory, physical, visual, creative, and self-nurturing. Once a child has experienced a variety of responses, you can ask what he or she would like to try.

For example: "Do you want to feel mad right now or do you want to change your feeling?" If your child wants to change, you could say, "What could you do? Let's see, you could run around the block, make a card to send to Stephanie, talk about the feeling, or read your favorite book." After you've generated ideas, let the child choose what works for her. Often all children need is to have their feelings acknowledged.

Be gentle with yourself.

Remember, some situations are resolved quickly and others take time and repetition. Hold a vision of what you would like for your child and yourself, and acknowledge the progress you have made.

Annie and Jesse were sitting in their room trying to be good. It was so hard to be good and quiet when it was their birthday.

Everything was exciting. The party wasn't until afternoon. There would be friends, presents, games, and food. It was hard to wait.

"I'm tired of waiting, Annie." Jesse complained to his twin.

"Me too," Annie agreed. "I'm so excited. I'll pop if I don't do something. Let's help Mom," she suggested. They ran to find her.

"Mom, we want to help," Annie announced excitedly.

"Fine," Mom replied. "You can help clean the bathroom."

Annie sprayed cleaner on the bathroom mirror. Jesse wiped it off. Annie sprayed a line on the mirror and said, "Wipe that." When he did, she sprayed again higher. "Do that," she challenged. Soon, window cleaner spray was all over the room.

"Annie, Jesse. Stop that! Now you have to wipe the walls as well the mirror," Mom said.

When they were finished cleaning the bathroom, Annie asked, "Mom, what can we do now?"

"If you can keep your mind on what you're doing, you can make tuna sandwiches. I'll work on the cake," Mom replied.

"Goodie, goodie, goodie," the twins chanted as they danced around the kitchen. As they made each sandwich they decided who would get it. "This is for Robbie," Jesse announced. "This is for Grandpa," Annie responded.

"No, I want Grandpa's sandwich," Jesse objected, as he reached to move it to his pile. Annie pushed his arm away and

knocked the tuna filling on the floor. The bowl broke and the tuna fish flew all over. Mom glared at the twins. "Calm down, you two," she warned, "or you'll ruin the party. If you kids *really* want to help — stay in your room!"

"Okay," they said soberly and went to their room.

"It's hard to be good when it's your birthday," Annie moaned as they flopped on the bed together.

"Yeah," Jesse said glumly. Then he started to think about the party and got excited again. "Annie, what kind of frosting do you think we'll have on our cake?" he asked.

"I hope it's chocolate. Let's ask Mom," Annie suggested. "If we ask nicely, she won't mind."

Mom was frosting the cake when Annie and Jesse arrived. "Hooray, chocolate!" the twins chanted excitedly as they jumped up and down around her. Jesse slipped. Both twins fell into Mom, and the cake fell into the sink.

"I don't believe this!" said Mom, exasperated.

Annie and Jesse stared at the broken cake. "We didn't mean to do it," Annie sobbed. "Can you fix the cake?" Jesse asked anxiously.

"I don't know, Jesse. I'll do what I can, but some things can't be fixed. Maybe we'll have to have candles on sandwiches or ice cream."

"Please fix it, Mom," Jesse begged.

"What am I going to do with you two?" Mom wondered. "I need to work and you two have lots of excited energy. You need to channel all your energy into something constructive. How can you do that?"

"I don't know," Annie said, looking at her twin.

"Do you want some ideas?" Mom asked. They nodded. "Well, I can think of five things," Mom said. "You could—

Do something active . . . . page 12
Talk to Grandpa . . . . page 16
Make placemats for the guests . . . . page 22
Have a Teddy Bear picnic . . . . page 24
Play a quiet game . . . . page 26

That's a lot of ideas. What will you try first?"

Which do you think Annie and Jesse will try first?
Turn to the page your child chooses. If no idea is chosen, turn the page.

Do Something Active

"Let's play tag," offered Jesse.

Annie saw her mother's scowl and added, "Out back."

They grabbed their coats and ran outside. "You're it," Jesse said as he tagged his sister.

"No, I'm not. You are," she said as she tagged him back.

After a bit, Annie got tired of running. "You're it. I quit," she panted as she tagged Jesse. Then she dropped to the ground to rest. "I'm tired of running," she said.

"Me too," Jesse agreed.

"Let's call Grandpa," Annie offered.

"Let's build a fort," Jesse said at the same time.

What do you think Annie and Jesse will do?

Build a birthday fort . . . . page 14
Talk to Grandpa . . . . page 16

Build a Birthday Fort

"Mom, we want to make a fort. Is that okay?" Annie asked.

"As long as you do it in your room, it's fine with me," Mom answered.

The twins hurried to their room. "You get the blankets, I'll get the chairs," Annie ordered.

Soon they had a fort constructed. They made so much noise, Dad came to check. "What are you guys up to?" he asked.

"This is a birthday fort. Only people who have birthdays today can come in," Annie answered.

"When you are done playing fort, you can make placemats for your guests," Dad said as he left.

What do you think Annie and Jesse will do next?

Talk to Grandpa . . . . page 16

Make placemats . . . . page 22

16

Talk to Grandpa

"Mom, will you call Grandpa, please?" Jesse and Annie asked together and waited as Mom dialed.

They held the receiver between them so they could both hear. "What are you two scalawags doing today?" he asked.

"Waiting," the twins answered glumly. "Grandpa, when you were little, did you get excited waiting for your party?"

"Of course," he replied. "Who wouldn't?"

"Did you get in trouble for being too excited?" Annie asked.

"Sometimes," Grandpa replied. "But I learned to avoid it."

"What did you do to stay out of trouble?" Jesse asked.

"When the weather was nice I would go out and run. Sometimes there was too much snow for me to go out so I would make up silly poems. If I was very excited I would imagine I was in a quiet place and let all the energy drain out."

What do you think Annie and Jesse will do next?

Make up silly poems . . . . page 18
Find a quiet place . . . . page 20

Make Up Silly Poems

"Let's make up silly poems like Grandpa did," Jesse offered.

"Birthday, Birthday, please come soon . . . " Annie began.
". . . If you don't I'll be a goon," Jesse finished.

They laughed together and Annie said, "You are a goon."

"I'm not. You are," he said and made a face at her. They laughed. "Let's try again. I'll start."

"Birthday, Birthday, hard to wait," Jesse began.
"Birthday, Birthday, don't be late." Annie added.
"We can find some things to do . . ." Jesse paused.
"While we wait for you." Annie finished.

"That's good. Let's do more." Jesse said.

"We can run and we can sing . . ." Jesse began.
. . . We can do 'most anything." Annie added.

"Let's tell Dad our poem," Annie suggested. Jesse nodded and they ran off to find Dad.

What do you think Annie and Jesse will do next?

Make placemats . . . . page 22
Play a quiet game . . . . page 26

Find a Quiet Place

"Grandpa, how do you find a quiet place?" Jesse asked.

"We lived in the country when I was a young boy. When I needed to calm myself I would go to a nearby stream and listen to the sound it made running over the rocks.

"When we moved to town, I found I didn't need the stream. I could sit in a quiet place and remember the sound of the stream. I would relax and let the extra energy drain out."

"But Grandpa," Annie interrupted, "how do you do that?"

"I get comfortable and let myself relax into the sofa. I imagine the energy dripping out my fingers and toes."

"Do you think we can do that?" Annie asked.

"Sure. Get comfortable. Imagine you're at the beach or someplace calm you really like. Then let your muscles relax."

Jesse relaxed on the floor. "This is great."

While they were still relaxing, Mom came in and said, "It's time to change your clothes and help me set the table."

Turn to page 28.

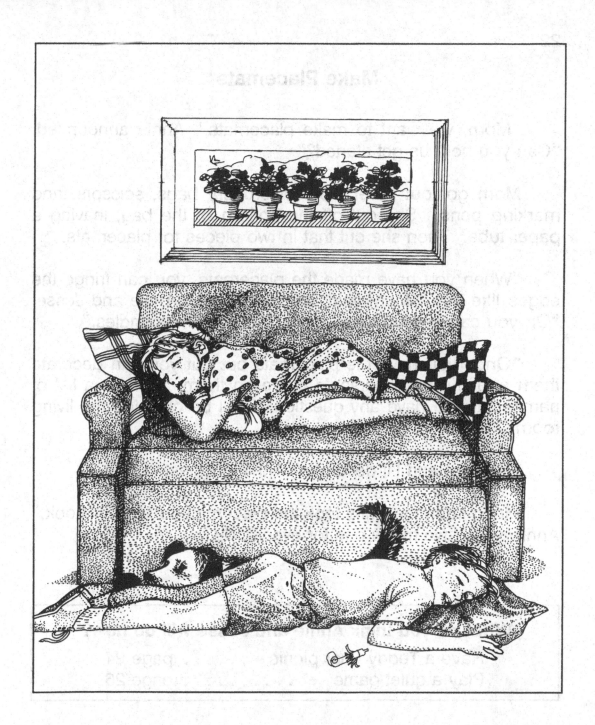

Make Placemats

"Mom, we want to make placemats," Annie announced. "Can you help us get started?"

Mom got out several brown grocery bags, scissors, and marking pens. She cut off the bottom of the bag, leaving a paper tube. Then she cut that in two pieces for placemats.

"When you have made the placemats, you can fringe the edges like this," Mom said, as she showed Annie and Jesse. "Or, you can scallop them, or cut zigzags like triangles."

"Once you have the placemats cut out you can decorate them and put each person's name on them. Here is a list of names. If you have any questions I will be cleaning the living room."

"You cut and I'll decorate," Annie suggested.

Much later, the twins took the placemats to Mom. "Look," Annie said, "we made one for everybody."

What do you think Annie and Jesse will do now?

Have a Teddy Bear picnic . . . . . . page 24
Play a quiet game . . . . page 26

Have a Teddy Bear Picnic

"Let's have a Teddy Bear birthday party picnic," Annie exclaimed. "You make the presents and I'll dress the bears."

"What presents would the teddy bears like?" Jesse wondered. He thought and thought. Finally he decided, "They like small cars and tiny plastic animals." He started to make wrapping paper to wrap the small toys.

Annie got out her doll clothes. "Ugh," she said as she tried a dress on the first bear, "this is too small." She laid out all her doll dresses and found they were all too small. "Jesse," she wailed, "what can I do? I want the bears to wear party clothes but the dresses are too small."

Jesse pondered a moment and said, "Make party hats. You can use my paper."

"Thanks," Annie answered and she began to make hats.

When they were done, they danced the bears around their room. And then they sang "Happy Birthday."

What do you think Annie and Jesse will do next?

Build a fort . . . . page 14
Play a quiet game . . . . page 26

Play a Quiet Game

Annie and Jesse decided to play a game.

"What shall we play?" Jesse asked.

"I don't want to play tag. And Mom will get mad if we play hide and seek outside the bedroom," Annie answered.

"Mom," Jesse called. "What can we play?"

Mom thought a moment and called back, "You might play Chinese Checkers, Old Maid, or Pick Up Sticks."

"Pick Up Sticks!" Annie and Jesse exclaimed together.

The twins got the game down. They flopped down on their stomachs. Jesse dropped the sticks. "You go first," he offered.

They took turns pulling sticks out of the pile.

Before they tired of the game, Mom came in. "I'm glad you found a fun way to use your energy. Now it's time to change your clothes and help me set the table."

Turn to page 28.

Help Mom

"Thanks for coming quickly," Mom said. "Please put the placemats on. Then give each person a plate, glass, spoon, and napkin. When you're done, I will put the food on. As soon as the table is set, we will be ready."

Mentioning food reminded Annie of the cake. She frowned as she thought of the broken cake. "I wish we hadn't broken the cake," she whispered to her twin. Jesse nodded.

The twins worked as quickly as they could. They set the table in two rounds. Jesse put the placemats down and Annie put a plate on each one. Jesse put the glass and spoon at each place while Annie folded the napkins just right and put them by the plates.

"We're done," the twins cried in unison.

"Nicely done," Mom said as she peered out from the kitchen. "Now I have a surprise for you. Fortunately I was able to patch the cake together with more icing," she said, as she stepped into the dining room carrying a beautiful chocolate cake.

"It's perfect, Mom!" Annie and Jesse chimed together.

The End

Idea Page

Annie and Jesse's ideas:

- Do something active
- Build a birthday fort
- Talk to Grandpa
- Make up silly poems
- Find a quiet place
- Make placemats
- Have a Teddy Bear picnic
- Play a quiet game
- Help Mom

Your ideas:

-
-
-
-
-
-
-
-
-
-
-
-
-
-
-
-